This book belongs to:

For my sister, Jane,
grandma extraordinaire, and for
Allison and Jamie and their teams
- J.R.

First published in the United States by Alfred A. Knopf, an imprint of
Random House Children's Books, a division of Random House, Inc., New York.

This edition first published in the UK in 2014 by Hodder Children's Books.

A catalogue record of this book is available from the British Library.

HB ISBN: 978 1 444 91811 3
PB ISBN: 978 1 444 91812 0

10 9 8 7 6 5 4 3 2 1

Hodder Children's Books is a division of Hachette Children's Books,
338 Euston Road, London, NW1 3BH
An Hachette UK Company

www.hachette.co.uk

How to Babysit a Grandma

by Jean Reagan

illustrated by Lee Wildish

A division of Hachette Children's Books

When you babysit a grandma,
if you're lucky. . .

it's a sleepover at her house.

What should you do when you get to her door?

Put on a disguise and say, "GUESS WHOOOOOO?"

Knock with a secret knock only she knows. *Tap, tap. Tappity-tap.*

If you like cats, meow. If you like dogs, bark. If you like goldfish, hmmmm. . .

When she opens the door, shout:
“Grandma, your babysitter is here!”

Hug your mum and dad goodbye and say,
"Don't be sad. I'll be home soon."

Now tell your grandma all the
fun things you have planned.

HOW TO KEEP A GRANDMA BUSY:

GO TO THE PARK

bake rice crispy cakes

have a fancy dress party

GO TO THE PARK to feed the ducks

do yoga

look at family pictures

GO TO THE PARK to swing

play hide-and-seek

make silly hats

GO TO THE PARK to slide

have a dancing-puppet show

read lots of books

GO TO THE PARK to take photos

do puzzles

play cards

As the babysitter, you need to let *her* choose.
Of course, she'll want to. . .

. . . go to the park.

WHAT TO DO AT THE PARK:

Slide down the bumpy slide and the twirly slide. If she's feeling brave, try *the tallest slide of all.*

Push your grandma on the swing, but not too high. Remind her to kick out her legs.

Feed the ducks. Show her how to help the shy ones get some food.

Don't forget: good babysitters always say, "Five more minutes!" before it's. . . "Time to go!"

Back at home, plan some more fun.

HOW TO PLAY WITH A GRANDMA:

Grab two microphones and sing a duet. (You might want to try "You Are My Sunshine" or "Happy Birthday".) Or make up a new song together.

Line up all her shoes to play Shoe Shop.

If your grandma likes fancy things, decorate her with ribbons, bows and stickers. Shout "Ta-*dah*!" when you hand her a mirror.

Soon it's time for dinner. Your grandma may be a yummy cook, but share your tricks to make everything taste even yummier.

Add sprinkles to anything. (Well, almost anything.)

Arrange the food to make silly faces.

Shut your eyes as you take each bite and say, "Mmmmm. . ."

Sniff
Sniff

When it starts to get dark,
take your grandma outside
to find the first star.

Back inside, snuggle up and. . .

Read some books. Turn the pages slowly so she can find everything in the pictures.

Ask your grandma for stories about when your mum was little:

"What was Mum's favourite thing to do at the park?"
"Did she ever get in trouble?"
"Was *her* grandma as fun as *you*?"

Teach her how to say
I LOVE YOU without
making a sound.

(Point to your eye, to your
heart, and to her.)

Now let your grandma choose where
she wants to sleep.

On the couch

In the big bed

If she asks, "Should we leave the night-light on? The hall light on? The door open?"

answer, "Yep, yep, yep."

Once you're both tucked in, make shadow puppets.
Have your shadow foxes kiss good night.

If she's missing your mum and dad,
tell her, "They'll be here tomorrow,
bright and early."

In the morning, when you
hear a knock, open the door
dressed up as. . .

TWINS!

After you're all packed up comes the hardest part: goodbye time.

HOW TO SAY GOODBYE TO A GRANDMA:

Let her borrow some sprinkles, some books, some stickers, some ribbons. . .

Say I LOVE YOU! without making a sound.

Give her a BIG hug and ask, "When can I babysit you again?"

More fabulous Lee Wildish picture books:

For fun activities visit www.hachettechildrens.co.uk